A BIOGRAPHY OF **MEMORY**

A BIOGRAPHY OF MEMORY

CHARLESTON THOMAS

atmosphere press

To my dearest and longest friend, brother and twin,
Ola!

'The music of memory has its own pitch,
which not everyone hears'

— Charles Wright

X X X

At the altar, I pour water, cool water. Ase!

Some hours after, I sit on an old mortar pestle permanently lodged in front of the sacred objects in my living room and contemplate the value of publishing this heavy pile of pages and ink in my hands. It's a manuscript: the re-worked version of my PhD study, some years after formally being awarded the degree. It feels like dead weight, that weight that tells when breath is removed entirely and life shifts into cold form, when bones become encased in dark brown rubber, taking on the bulk of coarse metal.

The living room contracts; the heaviness of the manuscript expands and fills the space, squeezing me into a corner of self-confrontation before objects and shrine. The thoughts that now flood my head have taken form as streams of perspiration on my forehead and beneath my armpits. The frequent and unrelenting bouts of doubt, anger and regret that had accompanied me through my years of living in the Big-Small Island, where the thesis was written, have now decided to manifest themselves as raw, frightful conflict as I hold the manuscript. Seems like the God of Confusion has paid me a special visit to school me in the art and science of navigating indecisiveness.

The 'book' has long been completed, but the only thing that's certain is my confusion as to what exactly to do with it. I had begun re-working the structure and content of the dissertation with an intention of having it published, shaping it into something that would appeal to the appetites of foreign readers, to satisfy the expectation that 'you need to put something out there'. But where is 'out there'? and what is this 'something'? Somewhere in the middle or towards the end of the bachelor's degree, I realised that what we were asked to read as students was not quite literature in a broader sense of the word, that is, written, visual, and aural/oral material containing the thoughts of a society. Rather, it was a miserly selected set of readings, either from the canon or the publications of some lecturers and/or their colleagues who have critiqued the canon. But because my appetite was so much wider than the required readings for courses, the idea of writing something that resembled this academic literature, by the time I was at the PhD level, was not an attractive one. In fact, the idea of publishing an 'academic' book — one that reads a certain way, one that uses a certain kind of specialist language, one that's written for a 'scholarly' community (otherwise understood as one that excludes the masses, including my family, my parents) — didn't at all figure as an option.

Yet, because my desire for writing has no doubt been fed by the tradition of my ancestors and elders on the Small Island, where storytelling was a way of life integrated into every aspect of living and interacting with people, I thought it might be possible to 'put something out there'. Aunts and uncles, village elders and church choir masters, carpenters and farmers, bus drivers and fishermen, seamstresses and village mid-wives all demonstrated a peculiar skill in having storytelling as part of their communicative repertoire. Some were more sophisticated tale-tellers, of course, relying not quite on accuracy either of detail or of memory, but upon the immense elasticity of imagination as well as on bending the details of an event or on replacing actual details with their versions of the happening.

However it was manifested, this tale-telling complex that had formed part of the rhythm of my growing up thus consumed me for a very long time, and a deep compulsion began to plant itself inside me, urging me to think about a sense of duty: duty to write something, perhaps to tell the story about the books and articles read and analysed to provide me with the thing called a PhD, or perhaps not to tell this story within the telling of my story of growing up with the arts and eventually growing into and away from academia. After all, within the academic fraternity, we are expected to publish something sometime after receiving the doctorate. 'Putting something out there' is paramount.

But this feeling of doubt and despair that is now plastered against the inner walls of my chest seems more than a feeling of merely being conflicted. This feels more like a kind of existential crisis, a crisis folded into desperation. The feeling of being used and exploited by the academy is now such stagnant water inside me that it feels impossible to get out. 'Drained'. 'Juiced'. 'Academically dead'. These are the descriptors that carefully paint my sentiments onto a canvas only my eyes and those belonging to Spirit can see. And this feeling of being academically dead has long seeped into the manuscript, adding more weight to already heavy pages. Yet, to be able to give back to my community through the act of writing, I must get past this inertia. I often wonder about the strategies soldiers with serious injury on and from the battlefield use to communicate the insanity of war, precisely at the point when they feel their skins sliding away from and off bones, when droplets of blood form footprints of rescue. From this place of thinking about the publishing of the manuscript, the desire to reflect on my creative history and pursue my creativity seems irreconcilable with the idea of flipping on myself and thinking about 'putting it out there', when 'it' is a thing that comes from a place of deep injury, anger, and perhaps love.

So here I am, confronted with desires of the past and decisions for a future. I remember the stories my father told me about how our family, 'D Briggs-Tamas Clang', emerged as popular village, island and national personalities through and in creative work. On several of our out-in-d-yard escapades with him, in the garden or with the animals, or in the gathering and cutting of coconuts to make coknut taat, coknut bake, and bajan, he would relish the opportunity he had with his children at his side to bestow the bounty of his knowledge regarding family genealogy, inheritances, traditional practices and so forth.

It was on one of those times when he was just completing the task of milking Lucky, our family cow, while preparing the bottles of milk that I would eventually have to carry to Cousin Leo, Baba Benji, Tanti V and countless others, when he reminisced on an aspect of his family history, telling all that he could to me and to himself. He revealed that our family (through his maternal side) had been doing creative work on the Small Island for over a hundred years. One hundred years, in my young mind, seemed like an impossible period of time for anybody to be doing anything, but when he started laying out the details mathematically, not only did I begin to understand how possible it really was, but I also realised that it was mathematics about me, a calculation of my years through the creative lives of other members of my kin. Almost in the style of a family biographer, he identified a few of his uncles, aunts and siblings and their dates of birth (and deaths when necessary), who were or had been village storytellers and musicians, historians, bone-setters and medicinal herbalists, midwives, blacksmiths, and craftsmen/craftswomen in the early 1900s. He shared, for instance, that his mother, who was born around 1904, was a singer, seamstress and baker; her husband, born 1900, was a banjo player. One of her elder brothers, born in the late 1800s, whom we called Uncle Rufus, was a well-known jazz musician and bandleader. He apparently was one of the many who had gone to Maracaibo, and when he returned, began infusing jazz innuendos into other folk songs on fife, violin and saxophone and was instrumental in assisting one of the island's most recognised anthropologists and ethnomusicologists in his research on folk and African-derived music forms on the island. According to Daddy, Uncle

Rufus was a big, big prapa music man.

In my twelve-year-old mind that day when my father poured history out to me, I began thinking that these artistic gifts were also handed to him and his siblings. My father, born in 1936, was one of the more recognised village storytellers, comedians, and historians and was equally a midwife and herbalist. His knowledge base was wide. From his mother, he had learned the high science of midwifery and thus was able to attend to his wife, my mother, and his two daughters, my sisters, as well as many of his nieces after they gave birth.

As a former captain of the village cricket club and an avid supporter of the West Indies Cricket Team, he was a local expert at the game in both its science and its execution. When I was selected by family members to write the eulogy for his funeral, I came upon an old sermon he had preached as an elder in the village church. He had used the game of cricket as the governing metaphor to tell the story of how love conquers everything, including hatred. 'Love' was the captain of one team, playing 'Hatred', the other team. The sermon proceeded to demonstrate precisely how each of 'Hatred's' players was bowled out, run out, or caught out, thus suffering a devastating loss to 'Love'. His style of writing was coherent and well developed, with a mix of inaccurate English with accurate Small Island Creole, and given his skills in comedy, the sermon must have been delivered with a bounty of humour.

His eldest brother, Uncle Tom (1926–2009), was our village bone setter, our church's choir master and a luthier. And their second-to-last sister, Aunt Flo (1938–1986), was a multi-instrumentalist and singer, as well as our church organist. In addition to the organ and the pan, she played the harmonica, the guitar and the piano. My father (with his wife and five children) had for a long time lived in the same yard with this older brother very close to our original family yard, where Aunt Flo, her six children, and her other siblings lived with their children. In this extended living compound, it was natural for us to gather and make music. Because Uncle Tom, Aunt

Flo, and my father, Uncle C, had converted from Anglicanism to Seventh Day Adventist Christians, and since singing and music were such an immense part of the church and the Small Island, it was their children who would either form smaller groups or who would rehearse rhythms for the church drum corps or songs for the choir. Those who played instruments such as the bugle, the trumpet, the guitar, the harmonica, or the piano would play together, do solos, or accompany those practising by voice.

The eldest son of my uncle was a very good singer and, with his father, led our regular Friday evening worship sessions. Four-part singing was the norm: everyone had to find her/his range (soprano, alto, tenor, bass) and then hold 'yuh note'. By the time I came into the picture in 1977, this was such a well-established activity that it was common for other families who were also members of the same SDA church congregation to join in on Friday evening worship sessions. We would either go to their homes, or they would come to ours. It was on one such Friday evening, as my father said, that I walked at the age of six months. My uncle's wife had me on her lap, and as the singing started, I jumped from my aunt's lap and fledged my way to my mother's. My uncle stopped the singing to utter his marvel at seeing his nephew walk at six months.

Years after my father's outpouring of this history, I found myself thinking about the artistic legacy of my mother's side. Though we were close with our mother's side of the family, the fact that we lived in our father's village with his siblings and their children meant that we were organically closer to our father's family. Nevertheless, I wanted to know what the artistic scenario of my mother's family looked like. I remember asking one of her older sisters one day who the artistic people were on their side of the family. She told me that my grandmother was a singer who sang solos at church, and her husband was a banjo player who played at a famous village rum shop. Several of their daughters, my aunts, were established church singers, soloists and choir members. My aunt, who shared this history, didn't quite have the same kind of detailed knowledge my father had, but she also mentioned that several of my grandmother's nephews became prominent musicians in calypso and soca on both the national and international levels. My aunt also reminded me that my own mother, which of course I was too young to properly reckon, had been an established village baker, having done the job of baking for the elderly for decades, and, although she no longer practices sewing, she was also an excellent seamstress who sewed Christmas curtains for other village mothers.

xxxx

As the day pushes towards its close, the memory of the expanse of this creative heritage shifts me into a re-awakened consciousness, but with the heaviness of the manuscript still weighing on me, I pour more water ... Ase!

> Night falls
> into the language of Spirit:
> 'reveal me only
> as your story ...
> read me
> through the fragments
> that punctuate
> and litter
> your story'

xxxx

The Following Day:
I leave for the Big-Small Island the following morning. It's a

short flight across, about 25 minutes. It doesn't take me long to get to the airport because my house is about five minutes away by driving, so I call an old friend to transport me, gather my things, and await his arrival. The heaviness of what to do with the thesis, memories of my family's stories and the directive from Spirit leave very little room for any meaningful conversation with anybody, and I therefore tightly hold onto silence, to hold and joggle the thoughts in my head on my way to the airport and to the Big-Small Island.

"Yea, man, blessings! Give tanks" are the only words I utter to my friend as I exit the vehicle at the airport.

xxxx

By the time I get to my apartment, a strange tiredness has hit me. This is not the tiredness of arduous physical labour that often times invites deep uninterrupted sleep. Rather, it's the fatigue of brain cells, that sensation of torment and unrelenting bother which hovers confidently in the corner of the head when doubt finds us. Sleep is a foe of this fatigue. The loudness of my thoughts amidst the haunting silence that now has me feeling so weary and uneasy evokes feelings to flee. I decide to go to the countryside up north to at least begin the final re-reading of the manuscript. This way, I calculate, if I can manage to complete the reading, I can then move to the next stage of talking to some friends about how to proceed with publishers. But the reading, I must get through.

xxxx

The North Coast

I get close enough to the farthest point up the north coast about four hours later. Bright early-morning sky blue transforms into a dark rainy day which does not at all worry me. A song list of Nina Simone, Billie Holiday, Miles Davis and Thelonious Monk plays quietly. It caresses the atmosphere and strokes me, like the rain, with raw, ancient vibrations. Before leaving, I had decided to play this long jazz playlist and to leave Ella Andall's songs for later. The jazz playlist prepares me better to meet and be in this moment. The van is parked just off the road at an angle, allowing me to see the river's release into the sea. From this vantage point, ideas of existence, of being African, of being Caribbean, of being woman, of being child, of becoming man swiftly conquer my head, urging me, strangely, to begin reading, however I manage to read. A dim overhead light finally decides to stay on, and I step into the drama:

XXXX

...

This thesis undertakes an examination of Caribbean men (their relations and their bodies) in Caribbean literature and gender discourse. I say Caribbean men because the focus here is on the Caribbean as a symbol of place and often a symbol of blackness. The study addresses the question of desire between black men as reflected in critical discourse and selected imaginative literature from the Anglophone, Francophone, and Hispanophone Caribbean from the late 20th and into the early 21st centuries.

In setting up the discussion around scholarly and imaginative discourse, I am aiming to achieve several things. At one level, the work aims to demonstrate how black male intimacy has been framed by Caribbean gender discourse, as well as to demonstrate how Caribbean fiction has portrayed black male same-sex intimacy and desire. In this case, I am paying particular attention to our critical processes of developing ideas for consumption in the university classroom and beyond. Additionally, in demonstrating how black male intimacy has been engaged by both academic and imaginative writings in the Caribbean, I am aiming to expose and outline, on a more general level, some of the major perspectives/arguments and literary frames in which male intimacy has figured at a particular time in the region's history. And in relation to the perspectives/arguments I try to outline, the work also suggests other ways of thinking about the role of desire in Caribbean fiction.

All these aims are motivated by one guiding principle: to contemplate other directions in which to take the study and writing on male gender relations. In this regard, the thesis provides extended definitions and applications of concepts, as well as engages strategies for analysing gender discourse and works of Caribbean fiction. Put another way, by paying careful attention to the approaches to defining and framing black male intimacy and desire in the Caribbean, the work re-evaluates the bases upon which definitions and categories of human relations and existence are established, and how our bodies are implicated by these very definitions and categories.

...

Throughout the thesis, I make several overarching critical statements. At one level, I argue that at this period in Caribbean literary and scholarly history (1950 to 2010), the region had been in a process of exposing more prominently the dynamics of male gender relations and male sexuality. However, male intimacy seems to have emerged more within the domains of sexual activity and eroticism. In fiction, there are either the erotic and sexual details of 'homosexual desire' or a tentative unveiling of the potential for male same-sex love and desire within a networking set of challenges. The study, therefore, discusses how the narrative structure of the literary work exposes the sexual and emotional realms of same-sex intimacy, and it discusses how this structure restricts the full operation and existence of desire within the stories themselves. Furthermore, I am suggesting that through this pattern of representation, male intimate desire emerges as a site for bringing more vivid portraits of 'non-heterosexual' men in the literary text as well as in the consciousness of the Caribbean.

XXXX

I raise my head from the pages. And look outside at the rain. It's coming down very hard now. The turquoise water from two hours ago is now thick, foamy, brownish wonder, still roaring, still turbulent. I go back to reading with the sounds of the rain, river and ocean lingering in my head.

XXXX

The study is organised around three central areas of argumentation, one logically leading into the other. The first general area of discussion is in relation to Caribbean gender discourse (its specific focus on male intimacy in the late 20th and early 21st centuries) and how such discourse has located desire as part of contemporary Caribbean thought. The second area concerns the literary text and its structuring and navigating of the principle of desire through its portrayal of male intimacy. The third area logically follows how male desire functions in the literary text both as an analytic and artistic tool in having us visually re-conceptualise the black male body in more complex ways.

These three central areas of my discussion are strategically stretched out into five chapters, the first of which lays out the tradition of talking about male intimacy within the academic context in the Caribbean. Three other chapters present different examples of imaginative approaches to engaging male same-sex desire and intimacy within contexts of resistance to colonial imposition, migration and revolution respectively. The final chapter invites us to take another look at how the language of male same-sex desire enables other perspectives from which to see and therefore asks us to think about the black male body in frames not ordinarily used for describing black maleness or male blackness.

...

XXXX

I think about this damn project of re-reading and publishing this thing in my hands. Left my homeland and my family, with so much music and creativity, to go to this godforsaken place called university. I light a spliff and turn up the music in the van. A Nina Simone version of 'Nobody Knows You When You're Down and Out' is playing, and it throws me into the memory of our music band, the then-most popular gospel music band on the island. We put on concerts, supplied background vocals to national and international artistes of renown, and provided music for weddings, funerals, graduations and more.

But this memory is a pathway to anger and resentment. Tormented by old desires to remain always in music, the already dim light within me that barely allows me to read wanes further, so to try and keep faithful to my commitment, I decide to head to a different location to see if the desire to do this reading will be stronger there. The Light House comes to mind. There I'll be able to see the distant silhouettes of the Small Island and read with fewer disturbances: there's no place there for other vehicles to come with their boom boxes on audio-display. I turn on the ignition, and start driving into the sounds of the rain. Billie Holiday now sings 'Good Morning Heartache', and I sing along with her.

xxxx

On this slow drive towards the Light House, my university years as an undergraduate student came rushing back, especially those awful classes in the Spanish Language. Spanish Literature was even worse, except with the only non-PhD lecturer, and Dr Ros, who, when she came, did a great deal to re-shape the programme into something more sensible and consistent. The non-PhD lecturer, Mr Kingston, was, for most of us, quite good. He taught us how to analyse character more deeply. I remember doing 'La muñeca menor' with him, and I remember this because remembering anything in the then Spanish programme is a challenge. Several of us who became secondary school teachers and gathered often for lunch or to journey on home together if we happened to be teaching in the same vicinity or school lamented having had little memory of authors and, more importantly, their scope and thematic focus, let alone influences and writing style. The French programme was different. Verlaine, Rambaud, Voltaire, Zobel, Condé, and 'Le Tartuffe' remain fixed in my head. I remember being excited to go to 'Analyse Literaire', one of the components in the French Language programme, and I always wondered why Spanish didn't have that as a component in its language programme.

Spanish, my major, seemed just a pure waste of my goddam time, especially after having come from such fine training at the advanced level in secondary school with 'Señorita' on the Small Island. It was she who had taught us the basics of translation and how to analyse sentences – with her 'sentence check list'. It was she who had taught us strategies to pick up the direction and sense of the novel and how to read and comprehend prose more critically by analysing sentences.

It was she, and my parents, whom I wanted to ultimately offer back my choice of sticking with Spanish as my act of gratitude. But in my BA Spanish programme, before Dr Ros came, and after Mr Kingston left, it felt like we were subjected to exam after exam, rush after rush, assignment after assignment, and very poor feedback and intellectual engagement at the tertiary level. It felt like punishment.

xxxx

I consciously make the effort to push back this rush of agonizing thoughts as I approach the road that leads to the Light House. For a moment, this memory that angers me gives way to my heightened adventure. I notice another trace on my right that leads into a large piece of earth sculpted by rain and wind to appear as if it belongs to the ocean. I surmise that on a rainy day such as this one, nobody's there, so I slowly I turn off the main road and onto this piece of sculpture. Thick mud demands a slow drive, which in turn invites me to take in the water on the trees that stand guard at the borders of the piece of ocean-view land. Water drains off the larger leaves, producing a series of instant waterfalls, all falling in unison, yet each drop individualised.

Although my aim is to get through a certain number of pages by the end of the day and I have some hours still to go, reading is becoming more difficult, more of a challenge. It's not that I'm tired seeing the words on the pages; neither is it that I'm wary of the content. It's simply that reading this thing seems to be reminding me of where I needed to be in life, to not have to face the ways of the academy. But alas, here I am, so I pick back up the manuscript and continue ...

XXXX

CHAPTER ONE: INTRODUCTION

CARIBBEAN GENDER DISCOURSE AND (THE PROBLEM OF) MALE INTIMATE DESIRE

From the late 20th century into the first decade of the 21st, Caribbean gender discourse has opened up discussions on matters relating to gender and sexuality. Within this period, a great deal of the discussion on gender has focused on sexual identities, sexualised bodies, the significance of the physical body and notions of the erotic. Drawing on earlier feminist legacies in Europe and North America, feminist scholarship in the Caribbean and Latin America from this period has challenged a number of issues, including questions of identity, difference, the conceptualisation of the nation and the notion of the citizen, specifically, the sexual citizen.

This chapter, therefore, follows some of the major perspectives in this debate on gender and sexuality in the Caribbean from the 1950s, with special emphasis on the last thirty years of the 20th century into the first decade of the 21st. My overall task here is to expose and critically comment on some of the ways in which feminist discourse has been pivotal in shifting the focus in theme and in critical practice in Caribbean scholarship. Given this task, I follow some of the strategies feminist discourse has utilised to encourage Caribbean readers to confront issues such as the exclusion of women and some men, and of other gendered and sexualised groups in contemporary society. In a more specific sense, the chapter examines the kind of critical space that has been opened up for talking about male same-sex desire in the Caribbean.

XXXX

Memory seizes me.

One lecturer in my MA programme demanded 'scholarly' writing from us. She said she didn't want to read 'undergraduate-style' essays. She also presented the class with examples of 'good scholarly writing': Hegel, Foucault, Derrida. Can you imagine! Hegel, Foucault, Derrida? What was asked of us would sound something like this: 'The inbetweenity of post-coloniality's excessive lament may refer to precisely the post-structuralist posturings which Derrida has theorised, and which the sporadic identificatory operations of postmodernity have set up as the discursivity of our time' ...

I take out another spliff I have, already rolled and ready to go. This memory deserves weed, wind and water!

This agonising thought and the already difficult-to-do reading immediately urge me into deciding to read selected segments from each chapter. There's no way I can subject myself to all dis Derridian, Hegelian, Foucauldian bullshit somting on dis ride. No, sa!

XXXX

Caribbean Gender Discourse and the Importance of Feminist Research

Gender debates emerging from the Anglo-phone Caribbean between 1950 and the first decade of the 21st century have been one of the major paradigm-shifting projects of this period. Given the focus it has had and the themes it has addressed, Caribbean gender discourse has set itself up to be and indeed functions as a kind of philosophical sifter through which the act of living and the question of relational existence (living with one another) become re-evaluated. This process of re-evaluation takes place in several ways: through more open discussions on issues relating to women and a certain category of men; through a different kind of visibility of woman-body; through the mobilisation of the principle of the feminine; and through the encouraging of non-hegemonic or non-dominant discourses. The complex mode of operation of feminist discourse is a direct reflection of the nuanced strategies (Caribbean) women have had to employ in order to navigate intersecting systems of exclusion and oppression.

...

XXXX

Reading this last bit has been a tumultuous task. This is painful memory. Conversations with colleagues about how to get published and the sight and sound of non-Caribbean lecturers begin to lodge themselves at the corners of my mind. Many of these so-called high-impact publishers have absolutely no interest in the genuine development of the Caribbean. Like many lecturers who keep coming to the University in the Big-Small Island in the name of Caribbean growth and development, hardly to genuinely involve themselves in village and community ways of making sense of the world, these publishers of 'high-impact' journals simply keep feeding off the wounds of battered but not fully broken bodies.

For the most part, they have no real interest in the Caribbean beyond that which advances their own academic careers and feelings of entitlement. And somehow, we at the University keep relishing the recognition their presence gives us. I've sat in on many a meeting to hear senior faculty make their selection of a lecturer based on the many 'publications' of the applicant. But where are these publications? Whom have they impacted? How is this so-called impact measured, tested? Was the applicant or chosen candidate assessed with Indigenous standards, or have the criteria for selection simply replicated non-Caribbean trends in hiring, thereby weeding out home-grown approaches to thought and the application thereof?

I'm aware that it is the reading that has uprooted this deeply troubling contemplation of the publishing industry; but I figure that the only way to blot out these thoughts, the only way to escape this vexing dilemma is to continue read-ing. For the only way to squeeze myself out of this trap is to know what to do with this compilation of pages. I must get through the reading.

XXXX

Contextualising Masculinity and Male Intimacy: Caribbean Literary and Gender Discourse

Of importance to this study is the fact that much of this attention to men has included a peculiar opportunity for the uncovering and examination of male intimacy through the domains of sexuality, erotic interaction, and masculinity. In relation to the context of Caribbean gen-der discourse, the discussion on male intimacy has taken shape in a particular way, where intimacy has largely functioned within the context of sexual relations, erotic same-sex interaction, or a particular brand of macho mas-culinity. I, therefore, survey some of the critical material related to male same-sex relations from the three regions in order to more fully track the geography of discussion on men in the Caribbean, particularly in relation to scholarly analyses of fiction, Caribbean music, and urban sites.

...

The discussion around non-dominant images of male intimacy in Caribbean critical discourse has swung between two extremes. On the one end, the discussion proceeds in relation to behavioural conventions established by heterosexual notions of masculinity and maleness, male sexuality, and male bonding. On the other end, the discussion takes place in relation to homosexuality and what is deemed homosexual behaviour. And it is this oscillating discussion that has, in its own way, encouraged an entirely new approach to thinking about gender and sexuality in the Caribbean. In the three regions being looked at, this theorisation and imaginative re-evaluation of the site of the male body, and male intimacy in particular, encourage new domains of study in the reading of both physical and emotional closeness between men.

...

XXXX

A few hours after, I get to a point where I feel myself settling more into the coolness of the evening, a necessary state for this laborious task. I contemplate moving from this spot to head to the Light House. It doesn't matter what time I leave to head back home. Many people are drawn to the warmth of homes and to the cosy setting of other places of abode when it rains. I've always preferred to be with the rain. Sometimes covered but always ready to be outdoors, somewhere in the countryside, to see rivers react to rainfall, to see trees drip, and to hear the sound of the falling water on the land. It's at times like this, like today, when it's wet and dark, when my mind travels to places known and unknown, taking me to the limits of my thinking. This environment of rain, coolness and darkness, with music enveloping the inside of the van, creates the right kind of atmosphere for deep reflections.

I get to the narrow road leading to Tantie Merla's, just off the main road, about six miles farther up, and closer to the Light House. Passing by Tantie Merla's road, the memory of all the times she took us under her wings, showing us, instructing us, and guiding us on how 'to save d chiren an dem' invites a slow and confident smile. 'When we marking fuh d people dem Inglish', she would advise those teaching in the programme, we should at least make sure 'dat d chiren dem wudnt embarrass dehself wit ah university degree!' My admiration for her as an educator was immense, and I was deeply humbled to be part of a training that would stay with me for the rest of my life. Through the teaching of how to write at the academic level, she taught us a whole world of how to show care and compassion for students: by telling them the truth about their writing levels and providing the facility for help and improvement; by showing us how to show more genuineness in helping students through a process of individualised error identification as well as by allowing them to recognise their collective writing challenges; by showing us how to remain as students ourselves in order to be effective teachers at any level, which is itself a lesson in humility, honesty and consistent hard work. She also showed us how to more effectively explain to students their (our) challenges in this business of re-producing something that's not our own – by showing us how to be considerate to students through legible production of comments and feedback that enable them to become more adept at self-editing and auto-didactic learning. Funny how this memory of Tantie Merla's training is triggered by the road that leads to her country house. Funny, not because it shouldn't have come back to me, but because there's so much more that could come to my head about Tantie Merla. Her work on the ground with community, doing the kind of labour not yet to be properly seen by many of those who now gallop towards titles and entitlements, with the clothes and the cars and the travel logs, and all.

Tantie Merla reminds me so much of the elders on both the Small Island and the Big-Small Island. Hers is a wisdom that is not merely birthed by books, like my father's, like CL James', like SCJ's. It's the mode of interactive living with the land, with and among the daily hard workers whose everyday existence is punctuated by disenfranchisement and disappointments, and anger and grief, and more anger and more grief, and indebtedness, and physical and emotional violations at unthinkable levels, and happiness and successes and joys – all this is what renders her activism and art (her writing and her teaching) so poignant and relevant to our living in the Caribbean.

I remember where I was when a mutual friend said to me, 'yuh know we hadda go een tong an walk wit Tantie Merla tomorrow. She sen dem a letta exposin deh arse. Well, boi, nuff people comin out to protest tomorrow against deh tricks wit dis constitutional reform ting, soh we hadda go'. With one carefully crafted letter addressed to the government and widely published in the print media, Tanti Merla became the kerosene thrown on flames that had already been burning among the citizenry, initially lit by government mismanagement, corruption and so forth. Tanti Merla's letter exposed the pattern of government dishonesty too long a part of the political culture in the country, and she inspired large numbers of people to go out and join an already planned protest against government under-handedness, lies, and deceit. The following day, she joined the marches, with a few of us around her for support, and remained there for 24 hours to make a statement as a citizen, all the while interacting with other protesters, helping to co-ordinate further action and, importantly, helping to organise food and sanitation. Naturally, being on this protest with her was itself its own training, and I also got to see Tantie Merla's more acute sense of community and civic duty.

My lesson that day was this: that she is a celebrated writer, academic, scholar, PhD, etc. – all the fancy titles that now lay the foundation for social importance – is of no consequence if the leaders of the country in which she is a citizen and which she helps to shape are allowed to be dishonest, bullies and thugs. So, funny it is that this memory, for instance, is not what came back to me as I passed the road to Tantie Merla's country dwelling. I suppose memory decides when to be remembered and where to insert itself, our heads merely the vessel and perhaps an endpoint.

XXXX

I get to the Light House, finally. The rains have returned, now with more force and clearly with an intention of lingering, forcing night onto the rest of the day. I'm slightly disappointed that the intensity of the rains and their accompanying clouds prevent me from seeing the Small Island, but I keep relishing the weather. From this spot, the long, ancient relationship the rains have had with the ocean and that now boldly shows off itself to me triggers images, abstract images of vivid beauty. I decide to put the music on pause for a while to take in more intently the conversation between the rains and the ocean. The mist rising from the ocean's surface draws me in to the interaction between these two magnificent forces of water. A meditative mood sets in. Before long, I drift into a doze and begin to wade through a disjointed dream about sea foam adopting the form of spirits.

XXXX

I open my eyes about an hour later and ready myself to read again. But before I begin, I pause to take in the ocean once more. Still roaring, she reminds me of the colour of the waters at Point Ikakos, the colour that had been the blanket for Kal and me on those days of our 'journeys' as we called them. She is now another transformative force before me, bringing these Ikakos moments into today's night and anchoring them in my head, these and other moments, deep in the forest, high up on the mountains, Kal and I with Miles, with Monk, and Nina, and Billie, and Ella Andall. It was at these times that I began to feel more deeply the desire to exit academia, moments when I felt myself indulging the mystery of possibilities ... when I was locked in thoughts of intimacy, isolation and music.

The waves continue to beat the large piece of rock that forms the lookout on which the van is perched, and there's a humming response to the lash of the waves beneath me. The larger the wave, the deeper the hum. This call-and-response vibration jolts me into thinking about the university, my father and my brothers. Ideas of desire, and desiring, and the desired swiftly make their way inside me. The BBC radio programme I had heard many years ago, 'The Heart ... and Memory', also finds its place among thoughts about desire and desiring and the desired. What had struck me on the programme was the conversation about the electromagnetic waves that we all have as humans, vibrating just off the surface of our skins, and that when we meet up with or are around people whom we love, these waves become more active, more reactive, more potent, more resolute on communicating back to us, the very fact that we love these people or this person. Microscopic equipment can show the dynamic reaction of these waves off the skin's surface.

Though more settled into night's coolness, I'm still deeply uneasy about this damn set of words I must get through, so I reluctantly decide to continue wading through the pages.

XXXX

CHAPTER TWO

DESIRE, BLACK MALE SEXUALITY AND (THE FANTASY OF) RESISTANCE

...

As is demonstrated by Caribbean gender critics, imaginative writings in the late twentieth-century Caribbean have been increasingly preoccupied with re-assessing and outright rejecting European/colonial conceptualizations of race and sexuality (among other issues). In particular, the trend in discourses of Empire to hyper-sexualise and eroticise black bodies has been continually challenged by Caribbean writers. This chapter examines one of the ways in which this challenge is set up by Lawrence Scott's *Aelred's Sin*. The discussion here concentrates on how black male homoerotic desire is made to form part of Caribbean anti-imperial discourse. I first expose how Lawrence Scott's work confronts the colonial sexualization of the black body. However, by pulling additional examples from René Depestre's 'Blues', I discuss some of the difficulty Scott's *Aelred* gets into in its rendering of a 'different' version of black masculinity via the trope of male homoeroticism. In this way, I am examining the degree to which black male sexuality and sexual desire function effectively as a poetics of resistance to models of masculine existence often framed as being heavily influenced by colonial thinking.

...

26

Desire as Counter-Discourse

In Scott's *Aelred's Sin*, published in 1998, male same-sex desire functions as an on-going system of counter-discourse, that is, as a narrative framework that counters colonial notions of a sexualised Caribbean. More specifically, counter-discourse may be understood as a structure of gender relations that undermines several conventions in Western-based systems of social order (such as the Church) and in the institution of West Indian/Caribbean literature. In this novel, ideals of male sexual behaviour as dictated by the Catholic Church, the so-called patriarchal nature of the Caribbean, and the religious codes of human sexual conduct in the Caribbean are all equally challenged and undermined. Importantly, this system of counter-discourse also emerges in the literary text against racial expectations and stereotypes formed by colonialist thinking and re-constructed by Caribbean anti-colonial discourses.

Scott's *Aelred's Sin* undertakes this challenge in a variety of ways. First, the novel sets up a notable counter-narrative to conventional and religious constructions of men and masculinity in the West Indian tradition. Then, and perhaps more significantly, it contradicts Christian and religious perspectives of male sexuality and male bonding precisely by situating homosexuality within the Church. Finally, the novel also undercuts the notion and imaging of masculinity thus far established in/by West Indian Literature. Its historiography of intimate sexual and erotic relations between men in the church is an intervention which has significantly modified the literary context in the English-speaking Caribbean. In other words, its publication in the West Indian literary arena meant that no longer could the literary tradition of the region be said to be merely hetero-normative since the novel brings homo-erotic visibility to act as a modifier of what we see of or know to be men's experiences of growing up in the 'West Indies'.

However, although male desire is set (and works) against conventions of masculinity and male love, this counter-narrative does not escape the very colonialist stereotyping the novel seems to be rejecting. While the novel can easily be said to be a graphic and bold challenge to religious constructions of male sexuality, male friendship, male love and erotic attraction, it remains trapped within the governing logic of colonial constructions of blackness. In other words, its treatment of the black male reveals the kind of prejudice and stereotype that easily accommodate the abnormalising of black/Caribbean men and of black/Caribbean sexuality, typical of colonial thinking.

...

XXXX

Ugh!!! What pain...to have to read these thick, exhaustive phrases and sentences.

The darkness before me now is midnight's darkness. But it's not yet midnight. Very quietly, Monk plays 'Naima'. I turn off the dim overhead light and the light on the phone, push the van seat back, and just chill. The trepidation that haunted me earlier in the day to begin the reading has somewhat subsided. But tomorrow is another long today.

xxxx

The Next Day

I awake this morning with the memory of Spirit's directive given to me back on the Small Island: '... only as the fragments of your story!' And so, today, I'll head deep south, the southern part of the Big-Small Island. It's the weekend, so traffic shouldn't be too much of a problem. I'll just have to remember to go further into my head while I get past the noise of the urban drive before I actually get to another one of my favourite spots, that place where Kal and I found sea stones and ocean mist, and the old wooden house, always seeming too far to get to, but close enough to tell of another person's desire for the sea, for earth water, for flowing currents, for the sounds of the night ocean, for peace.

But long before I get to this place of wonder, I'll have to get past many small towns, where car horns and loudspeakers, and sales and other so-called important audio and visual promotions, and the busyness of a hard-working 'middle-class', and the struggles of the vexed 'lower-class', and the flight of vehicles on this major connecting highway by government officials all come to over-announce our existence, traumatising the spirit of silence who lives in and by the sea, that bedrock of deep reflection! I'll have to get past all this. Well, not all of it. It's the weekend, so there should be less of it.

Some hours later, I get into the vehicle with a strong desire to remember my aunt T'Oves, my father's eldest sister and the first surviving girl of my grandparents. Not sure why this desire or memory has come to me so strongly, but inside of Ella Andall's 'Suite of Chants to Ogun' that has long accompanied me, I'm moved by rhythm and frenetic syncopations to ponder on her love for me, a love as strong and rhythmic as my mother's. My mind's wayward journey into my aunt's life sets me into a deep contemplation of the maternal principle: woman, the carrier and nurturer of forming and formed life, the bearer of the dead, and so much more.

My father once told me that she was born with all of her five senses, only to lose two from violent beatings one day by a primary school teacher. Physical violence transformed her for life, physically, psychologically and emotionally, hers and others. For many, she was by no means easy to deal with, yet for others, she was quite normal if *normal* meant confronting injustice and bullshit at the drop of a hat. Many called her warrish since she was the one to easily hurl obscenities whenever she thought she needed to, which, for her, was frequent. She was the one who openly cursed at neighbours and at family members so that, according to her, they would know that she 'naa play wid deh arse'. I suppose that's why she paid so much attention to schooling me in the art of verbal and physical self-defence. She would stress that the ability to get back up and fight, or to use the tongue to inflict wounds no physical weapon can, is especially necessary when in an already disadvantageous physical state. In my classes with her on self-defence, she would tell me, 'Nuh leh nuhbady chupit yuh arse ah worl ya. Gi dem tempo in deh arse'. Yet, her love for me was very tender, contradicting the other more volatile side of her, of which some of her own children and those of others whom she raised as a vocation were victims.

I always wanted to know her own version of the popular village stories about T'Oves, which as children, we all grew up hearing. One day I asked her one question, which seemed as if it was a question about everything. I asked her why people thought she was so warrish. Through the aggressive fall of tears, she told me of her experiences of repeated sexual abuse and of social rejection on various levels because of her disability, or because of talking 'funny', or because of talking an especially conservative Creole from the Small Island, or because she was a woman. She told me that of the 58 years she had spent in trafficking goods from the Small Island to the Big Small Island, learning the trees that fed generations and the land topography that formed the base of these trees, countless times she was treated with scant regard since she could not talk and hear well, so from very young, she had to go to another place inside her to bring out another persona who would be respected or feared for strength, for the use of her tongue and ability to fight physically. Her story is far too long and intricate for another narrator to attempt at detailing, but in short, she explained that some of her actions were clear and direct expressions of feelings of immense hurt and agony made tangible through sheer force, both physical and verbal. What is a body to become when it's the page on which abuse is paragraphed into a well-established and long cultural process?

Drifting away from thoughts of T'Oves, I realise that I'm close to the major turn-off to head south, that is, the major bypass to get into the southern part of the Big-Small Island. As I get to this turn-off, I'm struck by the crisscrossing imposing symbol that is this bypass, a metaphor for this grand internal shift in direction I feel, a clear yet unclear shift in direction, the direction to which I'm now turning to in my life. I know I have to get out of this atmosphere of animosity and pompousness at the university. Too many wear masks, and of those that wear these masks, many don't know who is behind them! Far too many are enslaved by a drunken hyper-eagerness to sell their work, their so-called scholarship, obsessed with titles such as Dr this and Professor that, Head of this and Dean of that! And although I know that the manuscript boxes me into a paradox, reading it over now is also the key to twisting my head in a different direction, back to a time before I began to breathe in this atmosphere, back to music, sacred music, to story-telling and poetry. Funny, the bypass to the South gives me deep satisfaction tempering yesterday's and today's trepidation; imposing as it is, it sets me towards a new path that is not new. It puts me back onto a road I know that I know, but what is ahead is yet unclear.

I get past the turn-off and pull to the left lane, a drive that is no doubt motivated by the sharp, abrupt sensation to stop and read ... perhaps it's the urge to complete the task, the eagerness to get this nagging part of my life out of the way. Within five minutes of my having passed the turn-off, I take the road on the extreme left, which takes me to the Bird

Sanctuary. And at a spot just off this road, in an area that resembles the clearing for a mega property, only that it is a natural clearing along the highway, I park the van in an angle where the bushes around the clearing cover the majority of what would be the visible vehicle from the highway. I place the manuscript on my lap.

XXXX

CHAPTER THREE

...

But however strong this desire, I can't read. I've tried to re-adjust the seat to see if a different sitting position changes this hold that keeps me from beginning to cast my eyes on Chapter Three, one final time. But it doesn't. I'm beginning to understand why I'm unable to read this chapter. I'm bombarded by thoughts of how difficult it was to initially understand what the hell I was doing in my first few years of writing this PhD. Back then, I had one of those long hard-cover large notebooks, where I stored all my thoughts and paragraphs on early chapters – I didn't yet have a computer, so my writing was done as I had done in high school: in a book and with pen or pencil. I initially struggled with incredibly abstract language, having had to swim through disciplinary jargon, in order to make sense of what I was reading and trying to analyse. But by the time I was at the end of the PhD, I had become known for being able to navigate the language of literary and cultural theory. I had developed the skill of breaking down the abstraction and using back my own versions of abstraction to convey their and my ideas. One day, a professor saw me at the very beginning of the academic year on the Humanities floor and said to me: 'I love the engagement you have with theory, but don't let them steal your voice'. This statement resembled the one Tantie Merla had made to me some years before about writing the PhD. She said, 'Boi, doh leh dem people an dem colonise yuh head'. Statements like these contain the sentiments of precisely what I feel right now. I have developed, it seems, this in-built resistance to so-called modes of respectable distribution of knowledge as well as to paradigms set up for knowledge acquisition at the so-called formal levels in the Caribbean.

Sometime after the professor made this comment, I began to think about how confused I really was by what counts for academic writing and certainly by what I seemed to have become known for. While it made enough sense for me to become recognised early on in my career as someone who was 'soaked in theory' or as the 'young and upcoming theorist', I was deeply unsure about how I felt about various academic perspectives that have shaped how education proceeds in the region. Furthermore, in my conversations with colleagues and emerging friends on Caribbean scholarship, several were struggling to express coherently, yet relished and fully indulged the confusion, otherwise known as 'scholarly writing'. My father had a way of describing and equally cautioning people who wrote and spoke in this way: 'Wheh yuh ah goh wid arrrl dem big wod, deh? Nuh bite ot yuh tong enuh ...'

How do I escape being colonised when I have to subscribe to the very rules that mimic old systems of control? Who has to sanction my publication? How much money am I to make from this venture? Why is there not yet a Caribbean Referencing and Publication Guide for me to be guided by, and why do I still have to go through MLA or Chicago or APA as the 'established' referencing and citation guides as a so-called Caribbean scholar, writing from within the region, writing for Caribbean audiences and with the legacy of the Caribbean university as the basis of my training? This steady flow of questions makes me uneasy. I've been at this spot for more than an hour now ...

I drive slowly back onto the highway, keeping on the slow lane, my body heavy with this rush of thoughts, which, like waves, folds itself and gathers more force, more thoughts, more weight to pour it all on my shoulders. Memories of my aunt's abuse pile themselves onto thoughts of the publishing industry and bring me more memories of other kinds of abuse I knew as a child. Internal bruises, blood, and fear.

Tears burst convincingly now, so I turn off the air conditioning and turn down the windows. The breeze from the outside hits my face and immediately starts evaporating stubborn streams intent on falling, on reaching my legs and the crease at the back of bent knees. Amidst tearful driving and remembering, I think about the feeling I get when I sing — that feeling of mystery, of wonder, of deep and immense satisfaction, a feeling for sound and melody and vocality and harmony and rhythm, and colour, and shades, and silences. A feeling that heals.

xxxx

I'm now in the Southland; the traffic is lighter, as expected. I see my old friend, the coconut vendor on the corner of Madrasi Street, who somehow always has good, rich coconuts. I purchase two, but instead of drinking them immediately, I stand looking at the sky. Its blue is the blue which wanted to accompany me to the Light House yesterday ... before the rains came. Today, though, the sky's blue reminds me of my visual challenges. Today, I can't look at sky blue for too long; transition lenses don't always help. The glare brings me pain today, as it so often does. Sometimes it's worse than other times, but there's always pain. Pain at the eyes, pain for seeing, pain for being able to see into the light. The pain makes me walk slowly into the shade under a massive tree, whose leaves soak up the sun. I sit on a piece of rock covered in light green moss, and the breeze hits me in the face, depositing dust. I squint my eyes to keep this dust out, but a stronger breeze follows, seeming to tell me to keep on my plan. Immediately,

I get up from the rock, bless up the coconut vendor, and get back into the van. Now, the urge to drink creeps in...

Back on the highway, the image of my mother leaning over the rails of our veranda back on the Small Island, the morning I took off for university in the Big-Small Island, comes to me. Like so many other women in the Caribbean, she laboured in the homes of other older women, helping to take care of them and their children and helping them to face their challenges and problems. In the late 80s, she worked four jobs and earned 800 Small-Island dollars, a total of four salaries, to take care of five children, having lost one, and the last, born not to see well. Like so many women in the Caribbean, she quietly but defiantly steered her own course on womanhood, Christianity and sexuality. It is to her enduring labouring that I feel most indebted. This is perhaps why I should publish something: because she worked too long and too hard to make possible my academic successes.

xxxx

Soon, I'm approaching a lonely stretch of road on the way to Point Ikakos, a long, lonely stretch on which I can smell the ocean. My driving is decidedly slower because my eyes are beginning to become teary from the early-evening's glare. I see a large mango tree whose fallen leaves are sharing space with young blossoming flowers. Although there's somewhat of a parking spot under the tree, I choose to stay a few metres away. I find a comfortable parking that lets me consume the majesty of the tree, turn off the ignition, and take in the moment, another moment of tree and wind and shaded sun. I reach for the manuscript on the front passenger seat and open it, but just before I continue the labour, a bird sings and calls my attention to its blue and yellow fluttering presence atop a branch that hangs farther out than the others. It tweets melodies written by an ancient composer, melodies which bring me a similar kind of calm that the ocean and the rains at the Light House gave me yesterday, and so, like yesterday, I put the seat back and turn the music off. Today, I take in the bird's song. Without knowing, I fall into a deep sleep.

It's about two hours later. Yawning away my sluggishness, I notice too that the bird has long gone. I get out of the van and walk closer to the tree. Its imposing, majestic trunk accosts me, freezing me for some seconds, directing and instructing me to observe its intricacy, its size, its magnitude, its unknown old age, its wisdom, its defence, its vulnerability. I breathe in deeply and sigh heavily at recognising my diminutive status before the tree, this elder who stands above and beneath me, showing me, if only I have the humility of time, how to live and search only for the right combination of nutrients for my anatomy and how to keep reaching for light.

After some long minutes of communion with the elder, I return to the van to continue reading ...

XXXX

CHAPTER FOUR

THE HOMO/EROTIC BODY AS POLITICAL WEAPON or THE RHETORICAL DISCOURSE OF DEATH AS NATION-LANGUAGE

If *Aelred's Sin* is concerned with the constraints of male intimacy in the Catholic Church and in the West Indies, and if Lafferière's *Comment* puts male intimacy on display within a panic-ridden narrative and textual structure, Arenas' *Antes que anochezca* uses desire and intimacy as the bases for setting up the marginalised male body as a political weapon. In this autobiography, there is a very expansive theme of homoerotic and homosexual desire, and such desire invokes the homosexual body as a political weapon against the construction of a masculinist nation-state. However, homoerotic and homosexual desire, in spite of its creative status as both defence and weapon against the state, remains trapped within a rhetorical discourse of death.

I am employing the notion of a rhetorical discourse of death as a communicative device of the homosexual experience and fate. Within the lifespan of the auto/biography, it is a discourse that is constructed by a network of images and facts, either of death itself or of inexistence from human community. A similar kind of structure of language and ideas is what also operates in Kincaid's *My Brother*, which provides additional examples of how this rhetoric of death is organised. In the context of the sexual citizen, the rhetoric of death is related to the contraction of disease, the impact of disease on the body, the thought and act of suicide, and the visual image of the medicine-dependent body. In the context of the writer, this discourse of death emerges out of the sites of exile and fugitiveness, which both mark a kind of inexistence from the national community.

...

The difficulty to map, define, confine or consolidate the nation can be traced through Arenas' autobiographical depiction of Castro's project of nation-formation. Arenas narrates his life in Cuba from childhood to adulthood, which is the period that runs from Batista's last years as President to Castro's seizing of political power in 1959 through to the formative years of the Castro administration. Arenas' life story, therefore, is located within the political milieu of the Cuban Revolution, and the nationalising momentum of this Revolution is what motivates the book's central story. Unlike all the other works looked at in this study, Arenas' autobiography brings readers to confront vividly the challenges of the sexual citizen within the context of anti-colonial nation-building.

It is, therefore, against the ideological construction and deployment of the Revolution that Arenas sets up his counter-narrative. This counter-narrative is a feat he achieves by detailing the evolution of a citizen whose sexual lifestyle and body mock and ignore Castro's 'moral' structuring of Cuba. The life that is exposed in his autobiography, now his vehicle of power, writes sexual desire between men onto the political landscape of the Revolution. Thus, while it can be said that the excess of heteropatriarchy (that is, the intensity of Castro's heteronormative and patriarchal regime and dogmas) is precisely what produces this rhetoric of death, it is the hyper-erotic and hyper-sexual make-up of the citizen that brings Cuban life into (autobiographic) form.

XXXX

I lift my head from the pages with a strong memory of the train ride to Canada, crossing one of the US–Canadian borders. I reluctantly confront the accumulated yet pushed-away pain of my years of foreign travel to do research for this study. On the train ride to Canada, I did my first reading of Scott in about four hours and took copious notes. I slept, ate, and looked out at the large farms and at one of the great lakes. That expanse of land and water overwhelmed me and pushed me back in the seat. I was stricken by the immensity of the earth. I remember feeling an unexplainably profound sense of home on seeing that expanse of land and water separated into something called the 'US–Canadian border'. Land and water, outside of our moving metal, brought a desire and a yearning for 'home', that place that is and that resembles Scott's Les Deux Isles, that place that had been causing me such distress. I suppose the lesson for me then when I sat in the train, as it is for me now as I reflect, is that home is everywhere and perhaps nowhere physically, but certainly inside of me, within these bone walls with blood and water and tears and bile, black bile, inside this casing, encasing soft matter, matter processing details and information and scents and sounds, matter that needs rest, deep rest for optimal functioning. I decide to continue reading to keep my head from going deeper into this memory, choosing, once again, the agony of reading over the memory that the reading throws back at me!

XXXX

Arenas first emerges in the book within the context of death. In this first chapter, entitled 'El fin', he describes himself within the last moments of life. Inflicted with AIDS (in its advanced stage) and exiled in Miami, he details his dying condition and his state of neglect. Beyond the portrayal of his dying condition and his migrant status, he introduces the idea of suicide, the very act that would end his life shortly after the production of the book. This announcement of the idea of his earlier planned suicide and the exposed condition of his disease-ridden body establish the site/sight of death as the introductory discursive context out of which is rendered the homosexual story. But this introductory site of death does not prevent the scathing attack that this very dying body/person makes on Castro's regime ...

XXXX

This bit has triggered another worrisome thought: the state of living of the black male in the Caribbean, especially the young black male. His life is so often shortened! He kills anything and everyone, including himself! He ignores or destroys his ability to become more wonderfully human because somewhere, somehow, someone or something convinces him that he is man, that is, exclusively male. By and large, he has been told and has come to believe that the woman is across there, on the other side, where tears are normal, where softness and tenderness prevail, where feelings, educated feelings, abound; he has been told, by and large, and has come to believe that he is on this side, where strength is supposedly contained in hardened faces, and where stifled emotions, uneducated feelings, form the frame of breathing mannequins, tightly concealed in suits, black, fancy, three-piece suits, clamouring for top executive positions, top political positions, top positions in all of capitalism's industries. And as the long narrative goes, these breathing mannequins believed they had the right to go to the other side, the 'softer' side, to take a woman's or child's body as it pleased them.

And yet, on the other side, where women apparently reside, this brand of the black male living in the Caribbean does not (or has forgotten) to see that it is right there from which he came. He does not (or has forgotten to) see or has not been taught that his emergence into a walking form was made possible by nine months of growing inside the belly of the other side; nine months of intimacy with the other side; nine months of listening to the cries of the other side; nine months of drinking and bathing in the fluids contained within the belly of the other side; nine months of careful breathing and feeling feelings from the other side!

I'm stuck at the thought of how many of us die every day. Men living in the Caribbean and elsewhere. We are born, and we die. We are born, raised into men and then begin killing women, babies, children, and other men. The clamouring for top positions seems a key thing. Somewhere, somehow, we have grown accustomed to the idea of man at the top, at the top of history, at the top of the business, at the top of the skies, at the top of the race, at the top of the salary scale, at the top of arms and ammunitions ownership, and at the tip of the gun. Alas! 'How Many More Must Die?' Haunted by this thought of black male killing and death and self-destruction, I consciously shift my thoughts back to the manuscript and continue reading. I jump ahead to the Conclusion.

XXXX

CONCLUSION

MALE INTIMATE DESIRE, LITERARY LANGUAGE, AND THE VISIBILITY OF DIFFERENCE

...

Sixty Years of Writing Male Intimacy in Caribbean Scholarship

The idea of male same-sex desire in academic and imaginative writings in the Caribbean between 1950 and 2010 has become more accessible to readers through varying yet connected ways of addressing male intimacy, that is, how men show love and express fondness for other men. Each of the chapters in the study isolates what have been identified as different ways of describing and defining male intimacy; yet, pulled together, the chapters move us to pay attention to the trend in locating male same-sex desire within the realm of sexual and erotic practice and potential. Discussions on male intimacy during this period are largely restricted to the business of sexual and erotic desire.

...

The various levels of closeness in the different patterns of male intimacy (including and excluding sexual intercourse) have not been substantially dealt with during this period, and therefore discussions and expositions of male same-sex closeness are almost always in relation to homo-sexuality. And it is precisely this sabotaging or, at the least, ambiguous dimension of our scholarship that this chapter has recognised as the 'problem' in talking about male same-sex desire. No doubt, at the turn of the century, we have been talking about men in (arguably) more critical ways than in the nationalist periods; but because our discussions have been so frequently burdened by sexual activity, the potential of our critical tendency has been inadvertently restricted. In this scenario, the politics of definition (of terms such as homosexual and gay) overrides the potential for talking more about how men show love for each other, how men intimately relate to each other, and how these dimensions of bonding work towards the strengthening of local and national communities, organi-sations, and the like. Discussions on the nature and useful-ness of male same-sex desire have been preoccupied with and thus stymied by a deep interest in sexual activity and the moral practices of the (erotic) body. Put differently, to many critics and writers , the term 'male intimacy' is a code for male homosexuality.

Caribbean Fiction and its Relationship to Male Same-Sex Desire

Within the context of the Caribbean Academy, Caribbean fiction between 1950 and 2010 provided much food for scholarly thought on male gender relations that have largely framed male intimacy as male homosexuality. The fiction from the region focusing on male intimacy opened up the debates around the male body and its acceptable forms of sexual and erotic existence in the post-colonial and post-independent Caribbean islands. Writers pushed boundaries in describing men's (sexual or non-sexual) rela-

tions with other men to the extent that they urged readers and educators to think differently about how to talk
about the Caribbean, Caribbean men, and the whole question of Caribbean identity. However, as much as they
pushed boundaries, writers of Caribbean fiction dealing
with male intimacy have generally unveiled a number of
intersecting anxieties, many of which keep the notion of
male intimacy within the domain of sexual activity and
which also sustain a certain pathology of black male sexuality and of the homosexual body.

...

XXXX

The small clock that's hanging out of the pocket of my bag
tells me it's a good time to go back onto the road if I want to
get to Point Ikakos and see the setting of the sun. And besides,
it's not too far from where I am now, so I can actually get
there and continue reading, and like yesterday, without any
interruptions. I'm told that folks don't like to go to the point
where Kal and I frequented. 'Drugs', they would say, 'Drugs
from dem Spanish an dem'. It may very well have been the
reason that we never met anyone there at that spot, but we
never complained, nor did we ever see these so-called drugs
from 'dem Spanish an dem'. What we saw, though, and certainly what today I am pursuing, was that large mass of water
that links the Big-Small Island to the South American con-
tinent; the sight of the seagulls dancing between the rays of
the falling sun and the water; the sight of the ocean, calm at
the centre, but rushing with force to kiss the sand, and land;
the sight of the evening making way for the darkness, the sun
taking its time to fall into the water, into the shadows of the
sea, into its nightly home, to slowly move and wait and then
emerge as the sun again, the next day.

Yes, this is the sight that I want to accompany me while I come to the end of this reading; this is the sight I want to see at those moments when my mind refuses to think about the pages I read but instead drives me into an attentiveness to the workings of nature. That's why I left home today for the Southland in the first place, just to see and be in the workings of nature. So, I decide to go back onto the highway and head to Point Ikakos.

On this stretch to Point Ikakos, my piano classes and Miss Weelah, my piano teacher, absorb my thoughts. She was one of those old-school, pristine village teachers of music. Under her tuition, I learned the scales, the keys, the chords, the fingering, the timing, the footwork on the pedals, the breathing, and the posture. I played 'Andante in G Minor' and 'Dolly's Funeral'. I did both practical and theory. At theory, I was horrible. I utterly disliked it. Too tedious and too un-musical. I needed to play and hear songs and play and sing along and feel the vibrations. I wanted to be at the piano all the time. Although I was excited to go to piano classes at Miss Weelah's, theory made music classes less interesting than they could have been for me. She was an incredible music teacher, and teaching theory was her duty. But I'm simply the kind of musical creature that needs to be in and inside of music all the time: its sounds, its silences, its nuances, not its theory on pages. My most significant memory from Miss Weelah was how she coached me to do deep listening. She would have me listen over and over to old tapes to get a fuller picture of a pianist's work. This is where I learned about texture and colour and sharpened my understanding of timing and harmony.

Miss Weelah's classes gave me the opportunity to meet up with other music students on the island who took classes elsewhere and did the same examinations offered by the Royal Institute of Music from London. However, seeing these other students didn't calm my own fears of doing these exams. Students from all over the Small Island, sometimes numbering up to 50, would gather at the library in the capital and wait anxiously and nervously to hear our names called to do our first piece, 'Sight-Reading'. This was invariably the worst part of my exam, since my dislike for music theory affected how well I was able to learn how to sight-read. What often happened in the 'sight-reading' piece was my getting a gist of the melody, and what I couldn't quickly follow in the playing, I would improvise. I would never leave a bar empty. Prepared pieces and those from memory simply flowed out of me. Miss Wheeler always said my musical memory was very strong, but I needed to work on theory.

Because these exams were from London, many parents who had students doing music in the Small Island were, often, more excited than their children, who had to take these exams, since the certificate from London was as crucial to going further in music as it was equally crucial to these parents' status in their respective villages and communities. It was always a 'good' thing to say that 'mih pikni geh e sortifikate fran Hinglan'. Fortunately, my parents didn't think much about this 'sortifikate'. For them, it was about getting me to do more music, which was the thing that occupied my attention for the most part of most days. Truth be told, it was my aunt, my mother's youngest sister, who was responsible for my learning to play the piano. It was she who had found me a music teacher, and it was she who paid for these classes. My parents were simply to ensure that I went to classes and that I kept on going. And they kept me going for all of my primary and secondary school years, just up until Miss Weelah's death, when I wrote examinations. By then, I had already reached grade four in practical, and before Miss Weelah's passing, I was about to take the grade four exam in theory, but this never happened since my piano classes ended with Miss Weelah's death. Just before her passing, I was about to re-write these 'important' final exams, and I was keen on doing well enough to be able to go directly into A-Levels, so my parents (and certainly I) thought that I could pick back up piano after exams or during my A-Level course of study. I did so about fourteen years later and began a process of hard practice and composition to be able to sing at the piano and perform, thereby re-claiming a portion of the Small Island part of myself.

As the memories of Miss Weelah and my time in piano classes deepen my understanding of myself and of my most acute desires I approach the last stretch to Point Ikakos, that long road that snakes its way through the community of coconut trees. I smell the ocean again, its salts, and the wind keeps bringing me small particles, throwing them at my face, arms and chest. I cross the bridge that puts vehicles directly onto the beach and slowly drive towards my favourite spot, that natural parking next to a fallen coconut tree. Here, I can use the tree as a footrest if I chose not to get out of the van, or I can use it as a resting place if I chose to take a nap, or I can use it for simply sitting and looking at the magnitude that is before me, compelling me to see its beauty, its raw power, compelling me to hear its sounds, compelling me to feel its mist, its welcoming particles, compelling me to taste its salted moisture, its coolness. I park the van, turn off the ignition, take some minutes to meditate and take in the presence of the ocean.

I reflect on the last piece of reading for a bit. Deep sighs and breaths leave my body as I sink deeper into the seat. Feeling myself going into the bottom of the seat, I hurl myself upwards and frantically jump out of the van. I'm sweating profusely, armpits drenched. I begin to understand what's happening as I begin feeling the contents of my stomach rising to my chest but refusing to rise further. The contents are carried in a heavy bag of warm, burning liquid . My eyes become teary, but I'm not crying, at least not consciously. My heart races ... chest burning, hand palms sweating, dripping now. A natural reaction to re-visiting my own experience, through

Scott, through *Aelred's Sin*, through reading about 'sin', through having to write this thesis, through having to search for and come to terms with the magnitude of desire. Contents all out now, my lips and nostrils forming the perfect topography for the cascade of bile!

Jolted by this expulsion, my mind races back to the abuse of the male, sexual and otherwise. This moment of remembering feels strangely therapeutic. Questions storm my head about boys' development into men. Seems like I'm repeating thoughts in my head, or, is it that I'm feeling the experiences of a past time?

Can all those men and boys whose bodies were used for experimentation and adult pleasure and hidden desires tell their story in a society that has come to only want to listen to how men cause the problems we live with? So often, some men's bodies are experimented upon and corrected through sexual and murderous desires; in colleges and universities and secondary schools and primary schools, our bodies are experimented upon through sexual desires however hidden; in families and in yards and in villages, our bodies are experimented upon by sexual desires however hidden; on the football fields or in tennis locker rooms or at swimming pools, our bodies are experimented upon and corrected through sexual desires however hidden; and in churches, congregations, court houses, judges' chambers, and other ostensibly sacred places, our bodies are experimented upon and corrected through sexual desires however hidden. In other words, wherever our bodies are available and open to another male (or female) who is supposedly 'in charge', in control, on top, d boss, big neighbour, once the desire is there, located firmly in the adult or bigger person, the child-body or another male-body perceived to be easily physically controllable is woefully susceptible to sexual access and violation and abuse and control. And it happens far more often than we care to talk about.

What does 'privilege' look like when it's the externalisation of deep insecurity? Or, when 'privilege' and 'dominance' are masks for sexual wounds and trauma, how do we give name to the scenario or situation or experience to speak its full truth, thereby recognising men's cries for help, cries that sometimes figure as 'male dominance'?

All this thinking takes a hold of me, still in the position in which bile was flowing out of me. Now done, I slowly straighten myself, reach for the bottle of water on the front passenger seat, and start rinsing my mouth while washing my face and nostrils. Trying to wash away these memories. The scent of expelled contents aggravates my sinuses. I must get this acid out of my head. I take in a generous amount of water in my mouth and rinse heavily.

Returning to the vehicle feeling empty, I place the manuscript on my lap. A strong breeze lifts the page I'm about to read. I'm at the bibliography. Once again, I begin to contemplate this manuscript the breeze wants to get out of my lap. It's heavy. It's over two hundred pages. Five chapters and a thick, comprehensive bibliography. Is this thing to be shared? How do I share it? With whom do I share it? And, if shared, if circulated, will it be read? And, if read, will it be understood in the way that it was intended to be understood? And if published through the channels of the academic industry, will these reviewing peers know how to shape the work for my communities, especially those in the Small Island?

xxxx

Night falls again, and I'm alone in the dark at the ocean's door. With sudden animation, I remember that the poems I completed editing a while back are with me. I remember that the last thing I did was to put them into categories. They are handwritten in pencil on another notepad. I turn on the ignition and reverse the van to respect the rising tide. Reaching for the notepad, I eagerly flip through the pages to get to the section on 'Poems'. I figure that somehow, this collection should, at the least, give me back something ...

INSTITUTIONS

Adrift

Proud
loud monuments
flags and sculpture
guide a quick pace
to their sacrifice
at the altar.

They drift.

Hoisted shoulders
strut along
in gowns
crowns
mimicking
the glow
of intellectual labour

They drift.

Frozen veins
inhabit floating shells
they mount
a playful theatre
never to resolve
the conflict
of performative posture ...
pastiche and simulacra

Adrift.

The Academy (of Bones)

Countenance of stone greets me,
cheekbones tighten,
contemplating
how to render
a welcoming smile.
Cold hands
dripping
with the sweat
of publications
pretend
to touch me.
But muscles dissolve
as they reach
to touch.
Sunken eyes
attempt
to smile
again
at the greeting.
Interest builds.
Shoulder bones
reach
a low high
and I,
still standing,
arms out-stretched,
see through
the hallow markings,
that shape
faces free
of flesh.

Mouths are open.
They never close.
'Call for papers:
Stories of self-formation and agency
of performativity and inbetweenity
of rootedness'

once
an old woman
told me
'the tongue
is heavy to carry
when the weight
of its story
is a fool's
open-mouth
thinking
that thoughts
are born
with mouths
never closing'

Audio-Visual

What do you see
when you see me?
Do my longing eyes
reach you?
When my mind
rejects the call
to buckle under
the weight
of your poise,
Do you see it?
Do you see it
refusing to bend?

Or,
do you just see
your long years
attempting
yet believing
to mould me?
Your time,
your haste,
seducing me?
Your greed,
desiring me?

What do you see
when you see me?
Does the crimson gel
that encases pupils

tell its story?
When night brings
her harmony,
enveloping me,
do you see?

Or,
was not your seeing
banished from
the city of beauty,
incarcerated by
and enslaved to
a duty
of deeply unknowing
the rich colour
and truth
of agony?
My chest feels
the flight of Gang Gang Sarah!
It explodes.
A thousand dialects
form at the mouth
bellowing hopes
and old women's
dreams to fly.
Can you hear?

Or,
do you
not only hear
the deafening chatter
of the long

dreadful justle,
that hastens
to taste
its own desire?

Soft

Against
Babylon's noises
I rest my silence.
I tell myself that
I am awake
only
to children's
sweet screams
and dreams.
And
to not face
the clatter
of Babylon's cities
I turn
to my soft
sleep.

When children's fingertips
find me
I am wisdom.
I know
how to sleep
a soft sleep
that rides
me off
into streams
of Divine Consciousness
– I rest my silence
against
men's wanton wants

with shouts and desires
that shock
life
from the dead

Babylon is not fallen.
But,
a soft sleep
brings my face
to night music.
Dew forms
on my nightly silence
sending fragrance
through my window.
Young
silent screams
of surprise
and pleasant dreams
fill the room
in my head.
I am
ready to live:
to not
face the chatter
of Babylon's cities.

For
there is
no clatter
at children's fingertips.
Soft
beauty
saves me!

The Search for Inside

Within the enterprise
of modernity's gesture
baptised into the bowels
of the everyday eclipse
I had found the folly
of youthful living –
head taken
by the mania of contortion
towards
mass belonging.
Then
one day
the blight of success
and the flight of pretence
flung my body,
hurling me onto ground,
compelling veins, muscles, and bones
to the beat of dirge

If
therefore
aberrant fingers
wrote the history
of long moments
of blissful toil
this woebegone meander
fitting for your disregard
was once, is still,
the stubborn soul's
seeking

to slip away
from tasteful bewilderment
and into
the pleasures of illumination
within Spirit's enclave.
A soul
stubborn for Spirit
knows eternity.

I breathe in these words as a conscious exercise of breathing out the university from my system. I figure that the only thing I can do at this moment, in this moment, is to spend time with the poems, to read them here at the water, here at Point Ikakos, here with the emptiness of my stomach, here with the heaviness of memory that has just been expulsed. With the rest of the poems, at least until I get to the very last one, Point Ikakos is my home ...

TIME

For Sanity

How
do I get past
this time?
How
do I keep
my head
from spinning,
spinning,
spinning
into the whirlwind
of the world's emptiness?
Do the trees or the breeze
or perhaps
the seas
save me?
'Alas!'
they lament
'Destiny of form enslaves'

How
do I get past
this noise?
'another person murdered ...'
'a new
fashion trend ...'
'a new
old term ...'

'a new
idea ...'
'another
political scandal'
– the rhythm of modernity's breathing
'another
economic downturn'
– capitalism's yearnings and failings ...

O Divine Song
whispering
beneath my skin
how
do I survive
the apocalypse of living?
Is it to be
in my dreams?
Then
give me more time
to dream ...
O Song
before she fell
Gang Gang Sara
flew
so
fill my flight
with purpose
Then
give me more time
to hear music
to see
falling colour

to hear
running Earth Waters,
Divine Waters,
trekking onto
designated pathways

How
do I get past
this time of too much?
screens of everything
including the richness
of the void
the vacuous
the vapid

I remember
when
in Morocco,
deep
in the midst
of night's desert,
I heard my blood
in dialogue
with darkness
felt vibrations
of distant beasts,
the long cry
of the night birds,
the silence of sand,
the night waters
that decided to flow
I remember

when
in Morocco,
deep
in the darkness
of time,
sky's blanket
consoled me
into another language
I felt
ancient time,
old time
Divine time
a time
long before
we learned
the sculptured smiles

When The Morning Comes

Sunlight glides
across my bedroom;
a bird pecks
at my window –
the morning
song has come!
Inquisitive breeze
peeps
through the cracks
urging
mundane objects
and shadows
to harmonise hopes.
A strip of yellow
plays solo
at my shrine –
ancestors
sitting still
welcome
the Sun's early embrace.

I turn on my bed
believing
in the morning song
that crept
into my head –
the melody for
the rage
of a day's gallop.
In my believing

I begin to see
a gentle living:
a tender exchange,
a labour of genuine reach,
a deep inward reach,
to know
the sweetness
of breath
In my believing
I begin to feel
my deep
inward reach
I reach.
I see children:
smiling,
laughing
consuming
Devine delight
learning
the language of Spirit;
and growing into humanity
This reach is deep

But outside
a sheet of chaos
spreads itself across
morning chords
waterlogged clouds
hover ...

The pecking bird
is gone

There's a shift.
Morning song
now a dim fragrance

Today, again,
the un-dead wrestle
tirelessly
with the un-done

What Happens ...

What happens
when I work
when I spend
the long nights
feeling
the fingers of the dark,
in the sweet shadows
of your presence?
Night flies
bring songs –
some in minor,
whisking me away
into the treachery
of remembering
how!

What happens
when I work
to melodies
of songs in minor?
What happens
when memory
becomes
sacred labour?
When memory
belongs
to the night,
when thoughts
of dark possibilities
shape the character

of the night?
Memory shines,
and I navigate
the corners of the night.

What happens
when night's silence
is the groan
of old diasporas,
a consoling groan
that writes
the bitter of lost hopes
onto the pages
of time?

That groan
is an ointment
to ingest;
ancient moan
takes my nightly labour,
refines boundaries,
and returns it
as refreshing taste

In this nightly labour
duty
is a long
solitary walk
a quiet song
to the Moon;
books and pencils,

lamp and light,
tea and thought,
insect songs
offered up
in reverence
incense smoke
and jazz,
night winds
and the blues,
piano and voice,
and dancing fingers,
laid at the Moon's feet,
and
at the seat
of the Stars.
And so
I drink
the soothing darkness
and enter
again,
into artful prayer

The Colour of Waiting

The closed yellow flower
smells the twilight
and beckons the night.
Before,
when green was her only colour,
she blended identity
into the forest floor,
marking her presence
beneath rubble and onto soil
that knew
the colourful transmutations
of herbs' ancestral labour and travels.
When her only colour was green,
she learned the transparency
of
falling
water,
and the bright yellow of energy,
piercing through the greyish whiteness
and the soft blue of sky
She grew.

Night is chemistry too.

When green was her only colour
the yellow flower
contemplated time.
She learned
the names of things
fallen;

and followed
their eager desire
to continue a labour of creation
directed and governed
only by time and night.
So before growing into yellow,
She learned the colour of labour:
the light of wind
shaking green and red
and purple and pink
and yellow
onto brownish ground,
giving to ground
the richness and wisdom
of fallen colour.
She grew.

As she grew,
she knew the colour
of groundwater,
learning how porous land
absorbs fallen colour,
how mist and vapour
paint white
the long flight
through time and night.
She learned that growing in the night
is black light,
a colour also produced
by cycles and repetitions,
and storms and volcanoes.
So she went through

the black light,
learning the white
of her tomorrows.

In her green being,
she learned
how tide and sea foam
rehearse again and again
their dance,
how silt and sand
deepen grey
at the river's banks,
holding in balance,
her breathing of time and life.
Understanding the divine pulse
of time and night,
the closed yellow flower
that once was green
stretches into her yellow,
overnight.

Today
she welcomes the sun's yellow.
Years of travels
through ancestral paths –
where ground and water
absorb colour,
where wind
turns leaves
on their side of white
at night –

reveal time's working
on the swell
of her yellow.

75

And still
more colour
awaits her ...

Moments

It is 5.45 in the evening.
I sit at my piano
and watch the mist of the Ocean.
The mass of greens and browns
that stretches
between me and the sea
guides my sight.
This evening,
The Ocean is cool light air
to caress a wandering heart,
to incite thoughts
about the sounds
that were made
to belong
to this mass
of greens and browns.

Thoughts become words:
"Boisterous cocrico duets exchange memories
of this season's ripened gifts.
Bird song invokes visions
of how to become
this moment."

It is 6.05 in the morning.
I am at my back door,
meditating,
and breathing in
morning mist and light.
Vibrant colours

shade my solitude,
And I stumble
into another thought
of this morning's
masterful happening.
Clouds form shadows
of old women
tending to the leaves
of this mass of greens;
and I see me
standing
among brown branches,
becoming,
this moment.

It is 1:19 in the darkness.
I hear night insects;
and a bold wind
brings another magic
of coolness to me.
the mountains I know
in the day
darken their greens and browns;
their silhouettes
hold my passions
against the starlit backdrop
of the silence
of clouds' passing.
They whisper to me
how to be
in this moment.

"Each moment is time –
time to reckon with
your fleeting presence
within the moment
of evening's coming.
You are caught in time's maze,
tossed between morning's muse
and the delightful darkness
of night's calling.
Each moment
of light and sound
amidst this mass
of greens and browns,
overlooking the Ocean mist
is time's insightful turning.
Each moment
of shadows and shades,
framing the day
and anticipating the darkness,
is time's shaping the
effort of your living."

Walk the careful walk
and surrender
to time's knowing.

Time is Memory

Time
walked by
my bedside
stretching its claws
into the flesh
of my anguish
dissolving the taste
of worry

I had lived
inside
the long slumber
with intelligent horror
teaching me
how to learn fear.
An acquired fluency
in thoughts of terror
supplanted
the excitement of growing,
yet formed roots
and branches
to keep me planted
in the macabre rhythm
of my living.

I awoke in alleys
to raucous sounds
and dissonance
effacing morning's desires.
And upon the fervour

to chance
the embrace of
awakened dreams,
fraudulent fingers
poured out
theories of distress
and doubt,
performing reason
and wit.

Pillows stowed
the torrents
of my torment.
Bed covers
pretended in softness
to remember
the promise
of reprieve
beneath night's caress.
I searched
the covers' tenderness
for light;
yet the day
kept bending towards
the clenching,
immobilising
charm of darkness.

And then I faced time.
Aromas of change
and the scents of seasons
pierced through

soft covers
and into
my memory.
A valley's language
infused itself in me,
educating feet
into flight.

In flight,
I began
to speak
in tongues
Once again
my body,
thrown into
the muse
of song
sound
and language
responded
to time's insistence …

Agitated, I remembered how to love
And I remembered how to remember.

Night, My Friend

Never
have you
withheld
your time
from me
tenderly
coaxing feet
into the chaos
of a day's passing
to be formed
and re-formed
beneath
the Sun's descent
into the night.

You never
falter
to offer
your dark
blanket of time
to me.
Soft coolness
finds me
urging thoughts
within
dew's erasure of seconds
within
the slow fall
of evening shadows

that extend
their lazy embrace
upon a day's sacrifice.

I am re-born
in the company
of your time.
The song
of your silent womb
sustains
the muse and moments
of my becoming
one with mountains
seas and rivers
beneath
dusk's unfolding

Raw and tender
your caress
is complete.
Old intelligence
of the darkness
carefully covers
my solitude.
Silence yawns
and I listen
to old stories
of the open space
to learn again
how to brace
the terror of day.

And
when all
this is over
you send in
the wings
on the winds
of slumber
to quiet
the contentions
and misgivings
of daylight's desires.

The Painting

Under the guide
of brush and hands
hues of yellow
converse on canvas
chants and off-beats,
improvise the backdrop
and this evening,
music is night
for the dawning
of delightful sight

This evening
blackened stanzas
that once yearned
to stain
the waiting silence
of the leaf
pour themselves
out on yellow ...
(many years before
a mind wandered
and hoped to discover
how ink and thought
can be brought into form
by the jazz
of Africa's overflow)

Soon,
as words melt
into the community

of yellows
as polyphony
and the wildness
of dissonance
morph and flow
into unhurried crescendo
when colour
receives
words' hopeful efforts
at making language,
meaning finds
more depth

A Head in Time

The head
that knows
its body
took the time
to learn
how to know.
It took time
to learn
how liquid pain
embalms the skin;
how tears
become words
to give
to the wind
that whispers
upon the layers
of the day
that shapes
evening coastlines.

The head
that knows
its body
dwelled within
time's hallowed distance.
Acquiring the art
of ignoring hours,
it walked past
frenzied betrayals
by hollow desires,

slighted minutes
of treachery and intrigue;
and instead
decided to embrace
moments,
to be carried
by birdsong
and by sounds
of the ages,
in order to be
present;
to be cast
into a knowing
that feels
textures and shades
and corners and curves
and dark places that
deepen the secrets
of scent and surrender.

In time,
the head
that took
the time
to know
its body
understood sculpture
and flow
breath and taste.
In time,
it knew
that molecules

and the dead
in their own time
provoke
the body's existence
into its forms
and formations

I make brief notes to myself about this section: "a long time to be confused"; "I should stay here for as long as I can, here at the waters, here in the dark"; "I wonder how long it took the sea to know what it knows?"

PAIN

Anatomy

You longed to see
what you couldn't,
you quiet eyes
and in your longing
and wanting,
a soft sound
came
moaning
your desire
to belong ...

A melody
fledged
and floated
and formed
the bones
that anchored
far-flung feelings
nestled in blood
vein and artery.

Quick feet
of your mind
scurried towards
evening dreams
and the shadows
of hope

in time
Fingers foraged
and found
ink and ivory
amidst the mellifluence
of your heart's longing
for not to belong.

My eyes behold
your heart
a
gentle
flower
ready
to
bloom
ready
to
fall
ready
to
produce
ready
to
reproduce
ready
to
nourish
ready
to
be
caressed

by
the
breeze
ready
to
be
kissed
by
the
sun
night
light
mist
and
rain
and
ready
to
bite
the
pain
of
knowing
how
to
tune
into
the
music
again.

Melodic Pain

O Pain! Sweet pain,
owner of my feelings,
You breathed on me
the weight of misery

Moods of a destitute humanity
carry me across time
to taste the sweet of bile,
to know existential bliss.
I inhabit a site
where song remembers loss;
lonely blindness is vision,
a ballad
amidst the shadows of a new order.
Wailing chords deposit grief;
beauty descends on strings.
They play quietly,
framing the technique
of a confident walk.
Vocals in prosody
gesture and pour honey
onto open wounds;
lilts and rasps
unearth the sounds
discover the inflections
of living within
the harmonic mystery
of Earth's refrain.

The Worry of Sight

The eye that does not see
wept that night
sending another
coarse worry
to shock
the twin
that bears the burden
of sight.
"What now, my love
when blood replaces tears?"

I'm suddenly conscious of this moment: the moment of being in nature. Long before today, I had planned to go the library and sit like a good scholar and pick through the manuscript with the best of what the academy supposedly gave me: the ability to read and edit and check and re-check until I see white then black ... blank. I had planned to brave the coldness of the library cubicles and conquer the welcoming drowsiness that overtook me once I sat to read. But yesterday, when I sprang into the desire to do the final read, it was only in nature that this re-reading could have taken place. The rains, the flavours of wet flowers and grass and earth, and the mist that blankets the air had to be the people accompanying me on this journey. The bends and the corners of the roads through light and darkness had to have been the pathways through which I would have to walk and stumble and walk again in order to be able to find this poetry ...

RITUAL

Balance

Here
on this desolate journey
where the lonely cry
of sound
walks with me
my weary feet,
heavy
with the weight
of worry,
take me
toward the breeze

Yet
While eyes pursue beauty
sight meets the bedlam:
    desperate desires
    excess of material appeal
    syllabi of strangeness
    programs of un-study

But cool breeze
swinging her long white fabric
through the trees
befriends me.
She lifts the dust
and I taste the beginnings
of balance

The dancer

Across the open waters
she danced
and the dust
at her feet
took flight
found me
bemoaning
the distance between
our feet

Where Beauty Abounds

The hills emanate
green confidence towards clouds
and from above
clouds reach back
to breathing hills
delivering songs of love

I see
the majesty of trees,
with buds,
moisture
and leaves
dancing the breeze
water
stores some of its memory
in dancing leaves
sap
slithers
silently
sweetening
sensations of green
sending me signals
that she
sits at the site
where beauty abounds

Birds chirp
the textures of desire
I hear
chords and harmonies,

layering open spaces
I feel
the splendour of night.
When silence
brings my head to the light
I am pointed
to the dance of her story:
'she carried
a basket of honey, fruit and flowers
to the river and danced
the Congo Bele
to the morning,
and returned
leaving footprints of old beauty.'

Then
I am reminded
'to see her, to be with her
is to see hills and clouds and trees,
to hear birds sing,
to feel the magic of night's sounds
and to be
where beauty abounds'

The Crossing

'... and then
             we
                   crossed
                         over.
No!

We did not choose the Crossing!

They dug deep,
deep
into
the divine
density of forests
a deep dig –
skinning and beheading trees that know how to live
uprooting roots
that know the wisdom
of Earth's layered ground,
bringing to all things
belonging to forests,
the chance of madness
to cross over

So
    all
        things
            crossed
                over
into
the

haunting
stillness
of the Unknown:
a barren site
where removal
and beheading
shock
and shock
is trauma
and trauma
is history;
all things
unceremoniously
driven
into
the chance of madness
in
the
stillness
of the Unknown.

The deep dig
into dense forests
found rivers and streams and springs.
Earth water,
sweet water,
Great Elder
giving life
to Land,
joining Land
to Ocean,
disturbed and burdened

by bleeding trees
and oozing cavities,
cried water.
Her soul and spirit
began

    a

      crossing

         over

into
a
long
uneasiness
telling
of its uneasiness
in enigmatic floods
and dried-up beds,
not ever
to be fully understood.
Sweet water
cried water
for those
who would soon
be taken,
sold.

The deep dig
found us ...
working, reaping, sleeping, dreaming—O!
Awakened
byimpatientbreathsandprofits,
by the disturbances of greed,
we ran, together ...

But greed does not relent;
the deep dig
caught us
some of us,
sighed
a silent sigh,
a final sigh,
together ...
Bleeding feet
left purple footprints
on Earth's ground ...
We walked,
not by choice,
together ...
Tied,
together ...
moaned,
together ...
We walked,
not by choice,
away from working, reaping, sleeping,
dreaming—O

Then,
we saw Ocean.
Then,
still tied,
our cries and sighs
turned guttural,
turned dark
Then

we entered, not by choice
small coffins
to restrain and carry
large bare, black bodies
Then
our cries and sighs
birthed new songs,
the beginnings of the blues ...
Then
we felt rain
and sun
and salt particles
and urine
and excrement
and blood ...
Then
with the help of the sun
blues songs and sounds
baked themselves
into our bones
as
  we
     crossed
        over
into
the
stillness
of the Unknown.

A new madness was born; but the blues is blue
with life and memory

surface blue
of the watery freeway
and un-lost particles
of the deep
restored memories
of how
to talk in Drum
of how
to return
to tones of the moan
to make the Crossing
into
the crippling
stillness
of the Unknown
that yet explodes
into today.'

Why Music?

Blue notes
erected a fortress
around a growing heart
tenderly cradling
the awakening
of centuries of stories.
And inside
the silence
of my heart's becoming
a voice was formed
and learned
to breathe
to receive
and give back
the wonders
of a life given.

Chords spread
a percussive blue
upon my head.
Indigo yawned a harmony
Enwrapping me
into cells and senses,
exploding birth
and movement
and thoughts
and wonderment.

Liquid tones
and colours unknown

whetted my taste
for the repeating
of seasons,
of Earth's tapping
rhythm – the dance of my mother's navel string,
inviting and dividing
limbs, yet forming

Fast and slow tempo
poured itself
onto my body.
 'The anointment'
I stretched myself
out in the sac
and allowed tempo
to flow

Blue hue
thickened by the swing
of indigo's song
readied itself
to see clouds
and taste the sun.
I saw clouds. I tasted the sun.

A song
carried my mother
and inside,
I sang along

The Wise Mystery of Children

Upon seeing the world
they cry a vast sound
casting loud resonances
into the firmaments
for the wind to take,
to carry to the source
and lay
at the feet
of waterfalls.

This cry is utterance:
vibrations
of primordial tongue
of life
arrived today
and yesterday.
It releases overtones
and echoes
of a long walk
through time, air and womb,
the walk that learns
the wisdom
of a mother's heartbeat,
yesterday and today.

Little feet grow
into a frenzied dance,
as they chase butterflies
and falling leaves.
This dance

of long memory
sends its silences
its dreams
and excitement
to the clouds.

When raindrops
make their way
back to us,
they bring
feet's dreams
and excitement,
sharing the vernacular
of bliss
of hope
of innocence
yes
raindrops share
the wonders of children:
falling sky water
is another light
that feeds
and brings
the beautiful becoming
of children's living

Eager hands
touch all
of Earth's giving,
theirs is an appetite
for learning
the delicate textures

of matter and substance –
feeding and bringing
like the light
of the falling sky,
the wonders
of children's growing.

From the depths
of their innocence
they learn
the gift
of sound
embracing
the elasticity
of voice
their voice
becoming sentience,
etches
in space and time
growing hopes
and bright desires
that tell
a thousand old stories.

Divine Intimacy

Mountains know
the skies
they touch
long cycles
of movement
deep
within Earth's underground,
serving time's demands,
assemble broad bases
to anchor
the character
and labour
of deeply feeling
a delicate knowing
of the skies
they touch.

This touch
is wild and selfless
mountain peaks
are never weary
to give back
to the clouds
the long love story
of growing
into Earth's core
discovering tales
of how diamonds
became trees

unearthing
and sharing myths
of how metal
danced with the breeze
mountain tops
never tire
in their desire
to touch
clouds and skies

Treetops
atop the mountains
dance the romance
of desire;
their roots
choreograph the dance
when mountains' desire
meets the skyline
old awareness
arranging
and synchronising
movement
of leaves and branches
at the skyline
is born
of a sensual search
that burrows
through plateaus
and topography
for soil's mystery
in nourishing harmony.

But trees
atop the mountains
that touch the skies
cannot dance
without the breeze
song
sent by the surface
of the seas
shapes the romance
of mountain touch
clouds
kiss the leaves!
skyline smiles
when the song comes;
for the breeze
is the song
inviting leaves
and branches
to dance
the kiss
of skyline
and the touch
of mountain tops.
Divine intimacy
inspires sight;
and
as daylight
gives way
to the cool blanket
of the night
soft, wild wind
awakens

a new dance
the silence of dew
excites
an old romance
to live this long life
together
of touching
each other.
Mountain tops
And the skies
they touch
mine
the moon's memory
for night's
returning delight.

Journeys

Kal and I, together ...
(just moments of incense smoke
fruit and water
wind and drizzle
and drifting salt particles ...
where two souls were sent to find desire
at the waterfront ...
where sand, driftwood, and seagulls
welcome the racing waves
rushing to kiss the land ...)

Night Bird

Last night
she sang
a screeching sound
piercing space
just at the limits
of contemplation.

The song
was an arrow
suspending itself;
determined to enter
the fractures
of thinking

Distant singing
ignited
flamboyant flames
sculpting pathways
of light and darkness

She sang
her screeching sound
into the lush brilliance
of the night
grooming the edges
of tomorrow

At morning,
when daylight's lips

reach the land
I stand renewed
ready again
to regard
the night

Deep Peace

I
descend
    into
        the
           depths
          of
          life's
          time,
falling
downwards
onto
hills
and
plains,
and into
trenches and valleys
that lie beneath
the wide water.

My fall is my surrender.
I aspire
no longer
to fight against
the colourless actions
of wounded desires.
Against the grey dullness
of insidious arrogance,
I throw
myself
into

the
downward
winds.
They place the sacred shell
around my surrender
and I feel
the hands of peace
taking
me
under
to
my
deep
release.

A vortex of light and luminescence
awaits me
in the deep.
The shining deep
is not
for total knowing;
but feeling (light in)
the deep –
       where bright men's brightness refracts,
       not knowing how yet to feel
       the weight of depth; and
              where colours of divine light
              radiate from the life
              that forms in the deep,
brings peace in knowing
how to bend
before life-light

and colour
way
down
under.

I am immobile.
foetal poise
forms my daily passing.
I feel life
under the Earth
and I smell roots
sea floor befriends me
the weight
of the water crushes
and I
become water
re-formed
to flow
beneath the waves.
I inhale the air
trapped in bubbles
that cluster
for a few.

Falling things
above the water
cannot reach me
directly
fallen hopes
no longer
accompany me,
for here

in the deep
I see
the light
of the darkness,
and effervescence
brings
        Deep
        Peace
        to me.

The First Walk

They walked
the treacherous walk
finding fire
and meaning
through the dark majesty
of forests
through night's pleasures
through the shadows of days
to create
paths for footsteps;
to find
life's long walks.

Bruised feet
scarred hands
the machete and the axe
found paths
towards
exchange and hopes
and offered blood
to the ground
grounding our search
for the marketplace –
the organising
of the desires
of our days.

Their walk
to the hills,
to bathe in green,

to continue
breathing the wisdom
of forest mist
created
pathways
for the walk
of humility and reverence

Their walk
to the rivers
to greet the Spirits,
to bestow
symbols and fruits
of honour and labour,
and to receive
the bounty
of sweet water's
returning
delivery
of herself to the sea
shone light
on the pathways
of sacred intent
a steadfast return
to the source.

They walked
through the night;
then became one
with the wind
that lives at night.
Night flies sang

a guiding melody
and they walked
with the wind.
They walked
the silent walk
of the dark
to find
the paths of possibility.

Cities were built
because they walked
and knew the texture
of ground.
Walking
the first walk,
left determined footprints
of blacksmiths and hunters,
farmers and storytellers.

They braved
the corners
of choice and consequence
cut
by trees
and streams
finding paths
of courage
to know
how
to walk
only
into the delight
of the unknown.

They walked
into the seasons
that temper greed
finding the key
to balance
the gift
of abundance.

Here at the waterfront, the manuscript is closed. No album
plays. The poetry now takes up prominence in my head, and I
begin to hear its music ...

THE TURN TO MUSIC

Many years after, I'm back at the piano. Because I kept on singing, singing on my way to teach, singing to the grocery, singing through the days of long travel in the rain, singing along to Nina Simone and Billie Holiday and Betty Carter and Ella Andall and Ray Charles and Nat King Cole, and finding the art of improvisation in Miles and Monk; and because I kept on listening, deeply listening to all the masters of blues, jazz, old gospel and Negro spirituals, and calypso and samba and bossa nova and Cuban and Brazilian Afro Spiritual songs, I sit now at the piano and wait to be taken on my journey.

I levitate and hear chords and patterns and repetitions and melodies and harmonies and rhythms and silences and hums and moans and groans and chants and scats. I don't hear a verse or a chorus, but I feel moods and see words. I scribble some phrases into the black notebook. They become the sparse lyric contained in the wide space of sound and song. "Meet me"; "Come with me"; "Let me be"; "Desire"; "Gentle Breeze"; "The Turn to Music". I feel the flow of the river and sea inside my body. I feel the curves and the corners of the roads. I feel the leaves that drip and fall, and I smell the wind. I feel the feelings of time pressing against my chest. My fingers are crooked and poised over the keys. My voice hears the masters, and I begin a long cry. "Steady yuhself," they say to me, "and sweeten the air."

The story ends with the Music.

soundcloud.com/charlestontmusic/sets

ACKNOWLEDGMENTS

Throughout the process of walking in this pathway, where wild ideas, passions and callings network to function as light that guides and prods and that sharpens intent, I remained deeply humbled by the magnitude of the task to consciously put vibrations out on paper and in the atmosphere. My choice to put words on paper in the forms of fiction and poetry, and my choice to add the other layers of singing and piano playing to written words, could not have been made into something tangible without a similar kind of networking of friendships and relations, all of which have fed this work in immensely significant ways.

To my Ancestors on whose spirit I have relied to feed my daily living, I remain at your feet!

My parents (Charles Thomas and Lilga Thomas), aunts, surrogate mothers (Ovethor Alexander, Vashti Thomas, Sylvia Collier), and uncles (Uncle Tommy, Uncle Jonathan, Uncle Stephen, Uncle Ivan, and Uncle Micah) who agreed that I was important to them and to this life thereby investing time in my care and development deserve acknowledgment. The relations they established between and among themselves in order to ensure I was well raised, as far as they knew how, are worthy of recognition, and I therefore sit at their feet... and make memory out of gratefulness.

To the community of women who looked after my head and heart when I began discovering the depths of life's challenges within and without institutions, I hold fast to your wisdom. Merle Hodge, Dionyse McTair, Sheila Rampersad, Jackie Burgess, Verna St Rose Greaves, Carolyn Allen, Folade Mutota,

Deborah McFee, Jeanne Roach Baptiste, Sharon Legall, Jennifer Rahim (in transition), and to my beloved sister, Danna Thomas, you have all held me as you hold each other; and this book is a reflection of your work on and time with me... so I make memory out of humility.

To my professor, Iyalorisha Jacqui Alexander, you have pointed me, spun me around, bathed me, taken me to meet and be with Esu and Obatala and Osain and Osun and Yemoja and Onile and Obatala and Ogun and Sango and Oya. You've listened to and spoken with me, and so you've marked my existence as real and as life...and thus I make memory by remembering how to remember.

To my brothers, who taught me the joys and bliss and value of male love, I have learnt more about desire from you than from any book or essay. Garfield Thomas, Anslem Akinya, Kai Leggard, Ngozi, Kwasi Nkruma, Kwasi Brown, Lyndon Gill, Damien Leach, Dwayne Garcia (in transition), your brotherhood has been my schooling on the layers and dimensions of male bonding...and so I make memory out of intimacy.

Special mention must be made of Councillor Tashia Burris, Secretary of Tourism, Culture, Antiquities and Transportation, whose support for this project and for research in general, have been invaluable to bringing this product to fruition.

To Atmosphere Press, who took on the task of meeting me, reading and re-reading my work, and making it possible to share fragments of myself in print, I owe deep thanks and gratitude. Kyle McCord, Nathaniel Lee Hensen, Alex Kale and Ronaldo Alves, you have carefully walked with me through the publishing process, and I therefore use your stamp on this book as the beginning of new memories and new biographies...

Finally, and most importantly, I recognise and thank my wife and step sons for walking with me. Xavier and Kobe, you have given me your attention, your laughter and the time to learn more how to be a father, and I am forever grateful to you! And Aquisia, my love, you have unconditionally cared for me and shown me the depths of love. You have shared with me your time, and ear, your mind, and I can never be thankful enough. Significantly, you have allowed me to go deeper into my spiritual and creative calling and together, we make music and rhythm and let our feet and arms dance the memory of our lives…

ABOUT ATMOSPHERE PRESS

Founded in 2015, Atmosphere Press was built on the principles of Honesty, Transparency, Professionalism, Kindness, and Making Your Book Awesome. As an ethical and author-friendly hybrid press, we stay true to that founding mission today.

If you're a reader, enter our giveaway for a free book here:

SCAN TO ENTER
BOOK GIVEAWAY

If you're a writer, submit your manuscript for consideration here:

SCAN TO SUBMIT
MANUSCRIPT

And always feel free to visit Atmosphere Press and our authors online at atmospherepress.com. See you there soon!

ABOUT THE AUTHOR

CHARLESTON THOMAS is a linguist, musician and writer from Trinidad and Tobago who explores combining fiction, poetry, the essay and music into one form. His academic essays have been published in Routledge Companion to Anglophone Caribbean Literature and Journal of West Indian Literature, among others, and he has done several performance-lectures as an invited performing artist at universities in the US, Germany and Trinidad and Tobago. In content, his recent work focuses on: the complex oral and African derived traditions of the Caribbean and their place in shaping contemporary education in the region; verbal and body gestures as part of Caribbean Creole languages; and on the practice, performance and value of reflective/meditative/sacred music-making in the contemporary Caribbean arts fraternity. These areas of interest are placed in his reflective essays and poetry, in performance-lectures and in music performance, in artistic productions, and performance-exhibitions.